A Fable about Miss Able

Based on the Survival of the first monkey into outer Space

Kim Pollock McGrath

A Note to my Readers:

This book is based on a true story! At the end, you will see the actual picture of Miss Able and Monkey Island as well as facts about her voyage. You can also find some short videos on YouTube about Miss Able, the first space monkey.

This is a tale that needs to be told, based on a real monkey who was brave and bold. A little Rhesus monkey that was named Miss Able, is the main character of this animal fable.

Independence, Kansas is where she called home. Her habitat was an island with a castle, this much was known.

Mickey Mantle played behind that big cement wall, gathering a crowd to watch the first night game of baseball.

The monkeys would climb up the castle and go through the windows with ease. They would swing on the ropes from tree to tree.

People would walk by; look, point, and stare. They brought bread from their homes that they would share.

Life was good and Miss Able was having a ball. But her attention was focused on that BIG cement wall.

She would wait until the dark of night, climb to the top of the castle and check out the sight. She clambered to the top and tried to see, but she was blinded by the lights flickering through the trees.

All of a sudden, there was a loud CRACK! The baseball was hit with a hard WHACK! Miss Able heard "MANTLE", then looked up to see, something white flash beyond the trees.

A shooting star, so bright and fast. Oh, how she wished it would have last.

The next day, Miss Able sat on the swing, lost in her thoughts about what she had seen.

Every day, Miss Able would wait to see if the lights came on from that big cement wall, then up to the top of the castle she would crawl.

She always saw the flickering lights but was waiting for the shooting star to take flight.

Without warning, a peacock landed by Miss Able's side. Noticing she was looking around with her eyes opened wide, she asked,

"What are you looking at? What do you see?"

Miss Able replied, "I'm looking for the shooting star to fly over me."

All at once, they heard a loud CRACK!
The baseball was hit with a hard WHACK!
They heard shouting of "Mantle" from afar, but Miss Able didn't see her shooting star.
The peacock was not the least bit impressed. He turned and left, gliding down to his nest.

Then Miss Able went to bed, dreaming about the vision of the shooting star she had stored in her head.

Days and nights seemed to go by, without the lights coming on and she didn't know why.

Out of the blue something caught her eye. She saw little lights gleaming from way up high. She saw one main light that had a beautiful glow. It looked so big from down below.

This was much better than the gleam coming from the big cement wall. The starry night had so many more, even though they were small.

Miss Able laid back, looked up into the dark sky, to see if there would be a shooting star that would pass by.

A surge of light jetted across the wild blue yonder. Miss Able's face lit up with amazement and wonder.

Oh, how she dreamed to go into space, being a shooting star zooming at a fast pace.

The next day some very important men appeared.

They were looking for a special monkey that had no fear.

They wanted to know if something alive could go to outer space and survive.

In the rocket the monkey would be placed, then sent off to venture in outer space.

One look at her and they knew, Miss Able was the one they would choose.

NASA

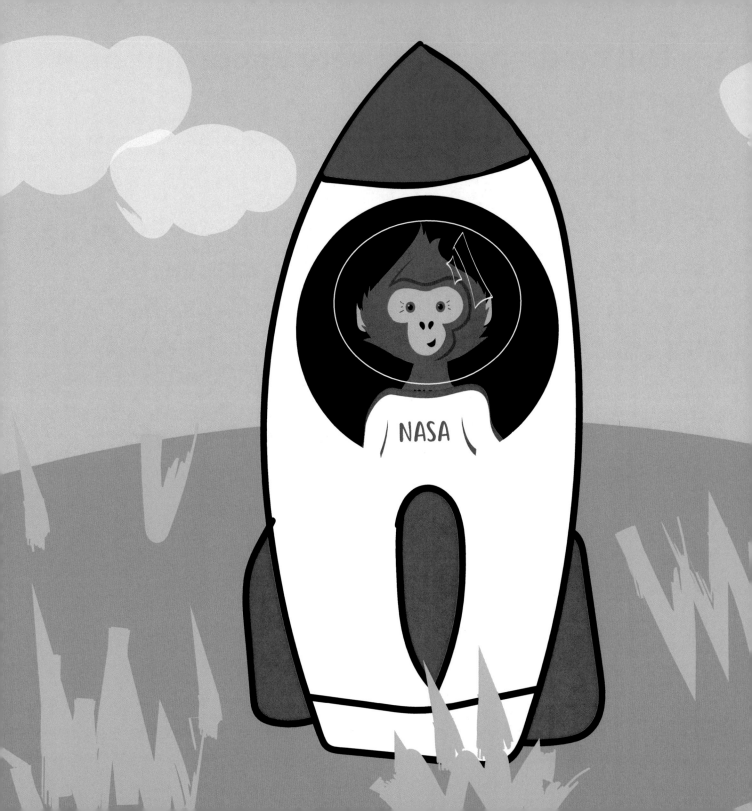

She was given a special astronaut suit that she would wear on her commute.

They placed her in the tip of the rocket, putting some bananas in her pocket. They buckled her in and closed the door.
The rocket started with a LOUD ROAR!

The countdown began...

10, 9, 8, 7, 6, 5, 4, 3, 2, 1...BLAST OFF!

The rocket progressed to 300 miles, while Miss Able was sporting a smile.

In an instant, the nose of the rocket detached itself from the sockets.

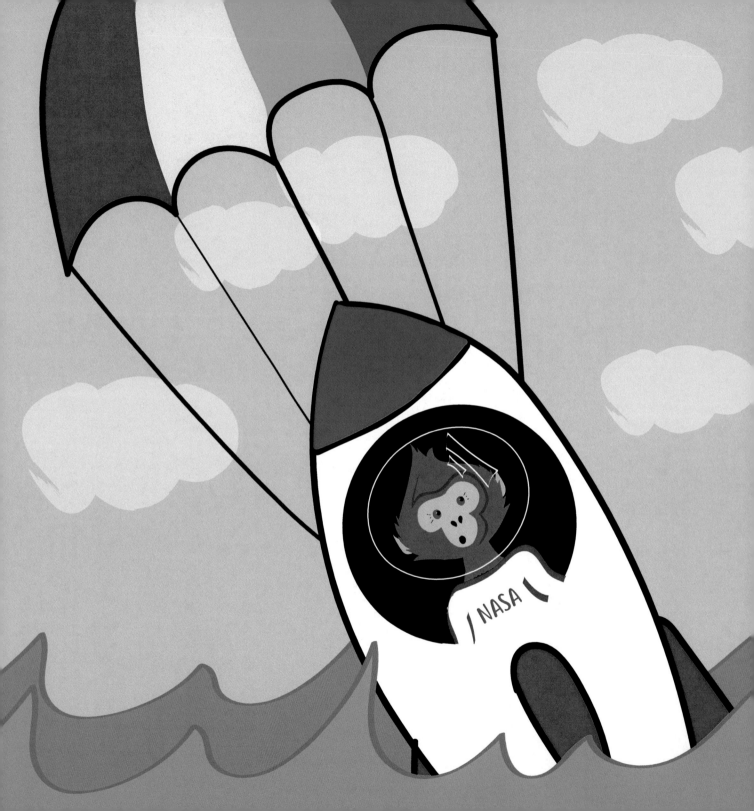

It took a plunge, decending down, then launched into the sea where it was later found.

So it's been told, that people looked up into the night sky and witnessed the brightest shooting star whizzing by.

She couldn't believe it!
Her dream had come true!

Miss Able...the shooting star..
that everyone knew!

Miss Able in Real Life

Miss Able, a rhesus monkey, was born in Independence, Kansas in December, 1957. Her home in Independence was Monkey Island, which is a stone castle on an island in Riverside Park and Ralph Mitchell Zoo. Located near Monkey Island was Shulthis Stadium, a baseball stadium where Mickey Mantle started his professional career with the Independence Yankees in 1949. Mickey Mantle hit his first professional home run on June 30, 1949, and it went over the center field wall at Shulthis Stadium. The ball was last seen heading towards Monkey Island, a distance of 600 feet from home plate.

Shulthis Stadium is also famous for another reason. The stadium lights that shined out onto Monkey Island first did so on April 28, 1930, the night that the first night game in the history of Organized Baseball was played. Miss Able actually saw those same famous lights in use since they were used for many years.

Miss Able went into space aboard a NASA Jupiter rocket on May 28, 1959. The rocket traveled 300 miles in altitude with a speed of up to 10,000 mph. She survived the trip into space, becoming the first American astronaut to do so. At the time it provided the best evidence that man kind could live in space.

Miss Able was on the cover Life Magazine in 1959. In 2009 Miss Able was a character in the movie "Night at the Museum: Battle of the Smithsonian", and is seen wearing her spacesuit with "Able" name tag. McDonald's later produced a Happy Meal toy named Able to signify her roll in the movie.

Written by Mark Metcalf

Monkey Island

Photos courtesy of Mark Metcalf

The real Miss Able

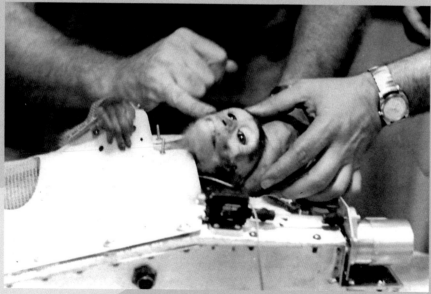

Photos courtesy of Mark Metcalf

Acknowledgements

I want to first thank Mark Metcalf for asking me to write a fiction book about our Miss Able, the first monkey to survive in outer space for her 60 year celebration. He also cheered me along this journey and gave me the non-fiction part at the back of the book. I thank Amy Bales, Eisenhower Elementary School Librarian, for giving me for some ideas and additions. Also, Anne Millis for always lending a listening ear. I thank Jillian Hagerty for illustrating the book and bringing the story to life with her darling illustrations. Thank you God, for giving me the storyline when I was stuck and of course Staci, who I know who is looking down at me and smiling.

About the Author

Kim Pollock McGrath lives in Kansas and has 3 children and two dogs. She loves hiking, exploring for little treasures, and finding river and sea glass. Her number one passion was basketball until she discovered her love for creating. Sharing her passion for reading and story time with her students, has lead Kim to become an author.

About the Illustrator

Jillian Jo Hagerty is a graphic designer and illustrator. Jillian graduated from Washburn Institute of Technology with certification in Graphics Technology and is certified as an Adobe Certified Associate. Her love for illustrating for children audiences began when she was an intern at Kansas Children's Discovery Center. Jillian looks for learning and adventure in everyday life whether she's traveling about town, across the country, around the globe, or through space.

https://jillianj0064.wixsite.com/website

Made in the USA
Monee, IL
18 May 2023